Where Can That Silly Monkey Be?

by Jodie Shepherd   illustrated by Steve Haefele

Simon Spotlight
New York   London   Toronto   Sydney

SIMON SPOTLIGHT
An imprint of Simon & Schuster Children's Publishing Division
1230 Avenue of the Americas, New York, New York 10020
HASBRO and its logo and PLAYSKOOL are trademarks of Hasbro and are used with
permission. © 2010 Hasbro. All Rights Reserved. All rights reserved, including the right
of reproduction in whole or in part in any form. SIMON SPOTLIGHT and colophon are
registered trademarks of Simon & Schuster, Inc.
For information about special discounts for bulk purchases, please contact Simon &
Schuster Special Sales at 1-866-506-1949 or business@simonandschuster.com.
Manufactured in the United States of America 0110 LAK
First Edition
2 4 6 8 10 9 7 5 3 1
Library of Congress Cataloging-in-Publication Data
Shepherd, Jodie.
Playskool where can that silly monkey be? / by Jodie Shepherd. — 1st ed.
p. cm.
ISBN 978-1-4169-9047-5 (alk. paper)
I. Title. II. Title: Where can that silly monkey be?
PZ7.S54373PI 2010
[E]—dc22
2009012247

Come on! Come on!
Are you ready for some fun?
Today we are going to the zoo!

Uh-oh!
A silly monkey has escaped
from the monkey house!
He is on the loose
and up to monkey business!
"Will you help me find him?"
the panda zookeeper asks.

YOUR TURN

**The monkey says, *"Chee, chee!"*
Where can that silly monkey be?**

MONKEY ALERT!

Can you find the silly monkey hidden somewhere on these pages?

First the pals visit
the wild cats.
The lion is much bigger
than Kitty Kandu!
The pals look all around
and up and down,
but they cannot find the monkey!

The lion says, *"Roar!"*

The monkey says, *"Chee, chee!"*

Where can that silly monkey be?

MONKEY ALERT!

Can you find the silly monkey hidden somewhere on these pages?

The tigers are
next to the lions.
Go Go Dino loves to look
at their stripes!
The pals look all around
and up and down,
but they cannot find the monkey!

Can you find the silly monkey
hidden somewhere on these pages?

MONKEY
ALERT!

The tiger says, *"Grr!"*

The monkey says, *"Chee, chee!"*

Where can that silly monkey be?

Tubby Turtle looks up, up, up
at the giraffe.
The giraffe looks down, down, down
at Tubby.
The pals look all around
and up and down,
but they cannot find the monkey!

The giraffe goes *munch, munch!*
The monkey says, *"Chee, chee!"*
Where can that silly monkey be?

MONKEY ALERT!

Can you find the silly monkey
hidden somewhere on these pages?

Digger the Dog watches
the dolphin play.
The dolphin leaps
high above the water.
The pals look all around
and up and down,
but they cannot find the monkey!

The dolphin goes *splash!*
The monkey says, *"Chee, chee!"*
Where can that silly monkey be?

MONKEY ALERT!

Can you find the silly monkey hidden somewhere on these pages?

Now the pals are
at the reptile house.
"That alligator has
sharp teeth," says Go Go.
The pals look all around
and up and down,
but they cannot find the monkey!

The alligator goes *snap!*
The monkey says, *"Chee, chee!"*
Where can that silly monkey be?

MONKEY ALERT!

Can you find the silly monkey hidden somewhere on these pages?

"Look!" says Digger.
"All the way up there!"
An owl is perched
on a tree branch.
The pals look all around
and up and down,
but they cannot find the monkey!

The owl says, *"Whoo, whoo!"*
The monkey says, *"Chee, chee!"*
Where can that silly monkey be?

MONKEY
ALERT!

Can you find the silly monkey
hidden somewhere on these pages?

The pals visit the kangaroos.
They see a joey riding in
a mama kangaroo's pouch.
The pals look all around
and up and down,
but they cannot find the monkey!

The kangaroo goes *boingity-boing!*
The monkey says, *"Chee, chee!"*
Where can that silly monkey be?

MONKEY
ALERT!

Can you find the silly monkey
hidden somewhere on these pages?

The elephant is huge,
from its big floppy ears
to its long swinging trunk
and its gigantic gray feet.
The pals look all around
and up and down,
but they cannot find the monkey!

The elephant goes *stomp, stomp!*

The monkey says, *"Chee, chee!"*

Where can that silly monkey be?

MONKEY ALERT!

Can you find the silly monkey hidden somewhere on these pages?

"Hey, guys!" calls Go Go.

"What is this I see?"

The pals take the monkey
back to the monkey house.
Go Go says, "I see *lots* of monkeys
looking at me!"